A De Rosthorn

On the tea cultivation in western Ssuch'uan; and the tea trade

with Tibet viâ Tachienlu

A De Rosthorn

On the tea cultivation in western Ssuch'uan; and the tea trade with Tibet viâ Tachienlu

ISBN/EAN: 9783742845382

Manufactured in Europe, USA, Canada, Australia, Japa

Cover: Foto ©Andreas Hilbeck / pixelio.de

Manufactured and distributed by brebook publishing software
(www.brebook.com)

A De Rosthorn

On the tea cultivation in western Ssuch'uan; and the tea trade

with Tibet viâ Tachienlu

IN WESTERN SSŬCH'UAN

AND THE

Trade with Tibet viâ Tachien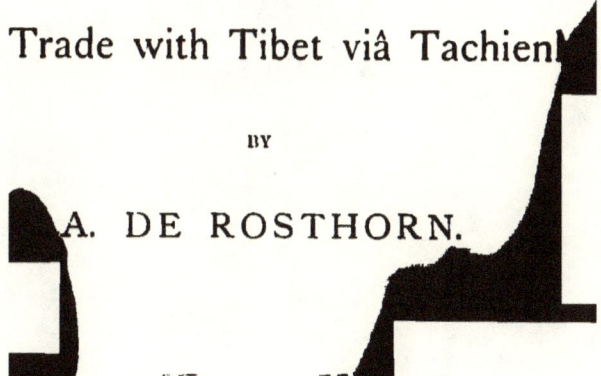

BY

A. DE ROSTHORN.

WITH SKETCH M

ON THE
CULTIVATION IN WESTERN SSŬC
AND THE
TEA TRADE WITH TIBET
VIA TACHIENLU.

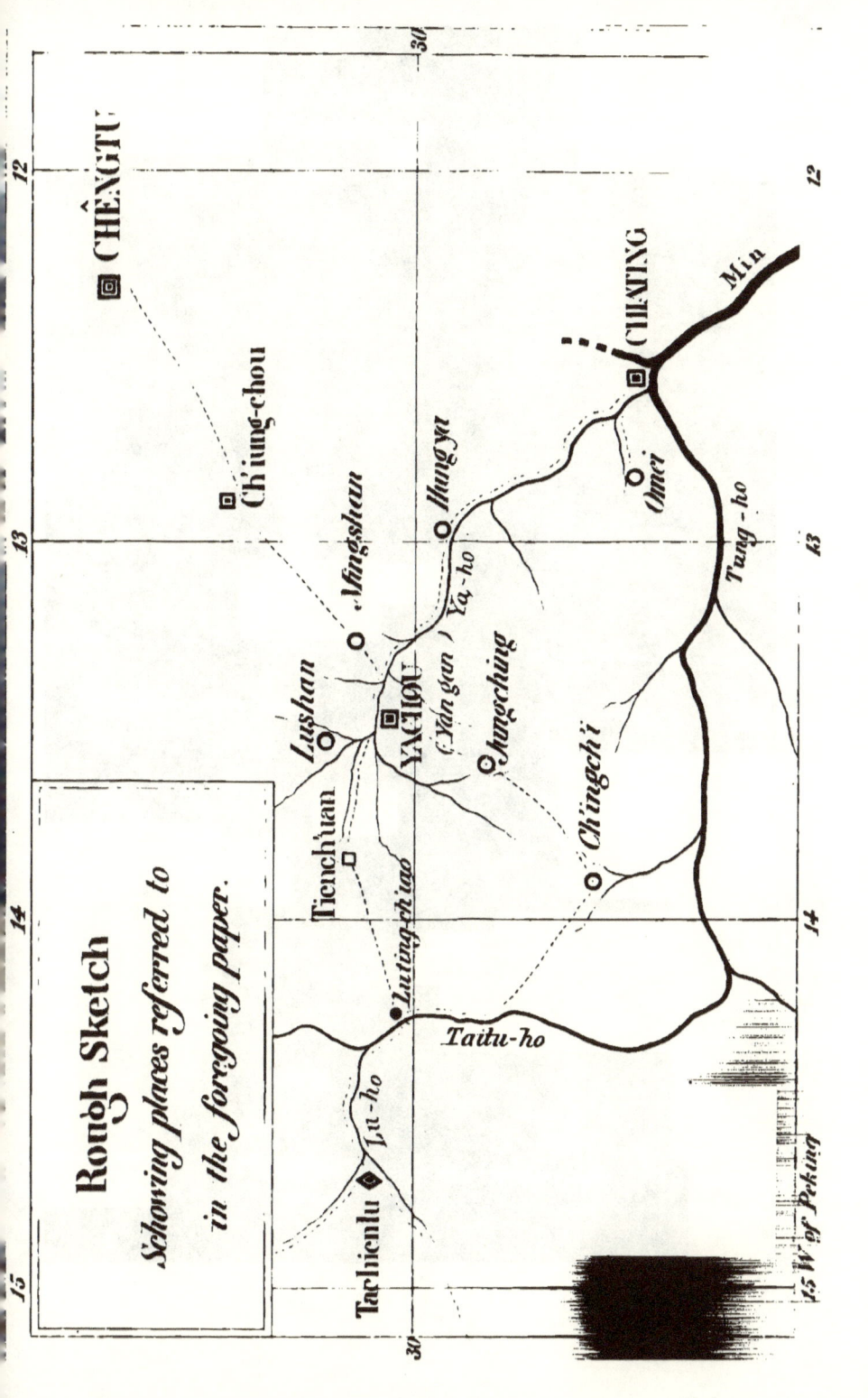

Rough Sketch

Schowing places referred to in the foregoing paper.

CHÊNGTU

Ch'iung-chou

Mingshan

Lushan

Ihungya

YACHOU

Yangün Ya-ho

Tienchuan

Chungchung

Chingchi

Luting-k'iao

Tachienlu

Lu-ho

Taitu-ho

Omei

Tung-ho

Min

CHIATING

105 W. of Peking

ON THE

CULTIVATION IN WESTERN SSŬCH'UAN

AND THE

TEA TRADE WITH TIBET

VIA TACHIENLU.

INTRODUCTORY.

The Tea Trade between China and Tibet, which takes place at the frontier town of Tachienlu, has attracted the attention of Foreign travellers since an early date. It is indeed impossible not to be struck with the endless caravans of yacks, laden with the elongated packages called "bricks", trundling along over roads which defy description,—if one happens to be travelling in the regions beyond that city,—or with the interminable chain of porters, staggering under their astonishing loads across two by no means contemptible mountain ranges,—on the Chinese side of it. Hence, from M. Huc who sighs "à ce qu'une civilisation corrompue et sans croyance a su faire de l'homme créé à l'image de Dieu, de l'homme presque égal aux anges", etc., (L'Empire Chinois, I. p. 17), down to Mr. W. W. Rockhill, the latest explorer in these parts (The Land of the Lamas p. 277

every traveller has gone into the subject more or less deeply, and a great deal of valuable information has been gathered in this manner, especially by the Abbé Desgodins and Messrs. Baber and Rockhill.

Remarkable, however, as must be in every respect a trade, which is carried on under such enormous difficulties and yet apparently with so much success, it has become of late years a subject of more than ordinary interest on account of the commercial and political questions it involves.   It was a pet theme with the late Mr. Baber, one of the shrewdest observers and most amiable of writers, that Tibet, preeminently a tea consuming country, should, by right of contiguity, be supplied with that staple from Assam, or India generally.   It is true that, latterly, through the enquiries of Mr. Rockhill and others, the opinion has gained ground, that the Indian teas are unsuited, or not as well suited as the Chinese product, for the consumption in Tibet, owing to their greater astringency and headiness (The Land of the Lamas, p. 281, Note 2); but, the hope of being able yet to supersede China in her commercial supremacy in Tibet, which rests entirely on the tea trade, and perhaps the knowledge also, that the commercial dependence of that country is a political lever of no small importance, have no doubt made the opening of Tibet on the Indian side to appear to Englishmen highly desirable, while to the Chinese they have furnished an excellent pretext, if not a powerful motive, for refusing their assent to any proposals in that direction.

I have before me quite a literature on the subject under discussion. The figures contained in the various reports and papers however, though sometimes remarkably near the truth, are, mere guesses or fragments of verbal information. In 1891, when I made the journey from Tachienlu viâ T'iench'uan to Yachou, I had opportunities for observing the more outward and ostensible features of the trade; and, continuing to pursue the subject afterwards, I was able, through exceptional facilities, to bring together sundry details not hitherto commonly known, as well as statistics which, though partly anticipated, are at any rate well authenticated and entirely trustworthy. These I am now induced to publish in the hope that, under the circumstances alluded to, they may prove opportune and interesting.

A question of purely theoretical interest, which had occupied me even before I started on my journey, is, whether the tea plant does or does not grow wild in Western Ssuch'uan. Various passages occurring in both native and foreign works (Cooper, Baber, Gill) had led me to suspect that it does. That shrubs, if neglected and overgrown, may "run wild" in a soil and climate so favourable to their growth, is highly probable. We must also leave out of consideration those curious groceries mentioned by Mr. Baber at the end of his paper, the sweet variety *(t'ien-ch'a)* sold on Mount Omei, and the white tea *(pe-ch'a* or *hsüe-ch'a)* also mentioned by Mr. Rockhill (Loc. cit.),—the former, because it is simply a deception practised by the priests, who soak the ordinary tea leaves in a solution of sugar before roasting them; the latter, because it is not tea at all, but a kind of lichen of local occurrence. The question then remains, whether the ordinary tea plant does or does not belong to the indigenous flora of the region referred to. I can only say that I have seen none growing wild, and that all the enquiries I made tend to confirm my observation. It is true, as will be seen, that the "tea" made up for the Tibetan market, consists but for the smallest part of genuine tea leaf; but the brushwood employed for admixture, which is probably responsible for the "wild tea" theory, is composed simply of the leaves and branches of certain shrubs and trees which, like the scrub oak, vitex, and others, lend themselves to the adulteration, and for the existence in a wild state of the genuine tea plant there seems to be no evidence whatever.

With regard to the domestic tea shrub, again, it will be observed later on that its cultivation for seed, and the art of laying out plantations, are secrets and monopolies of the inhabitants of Mingshan and Yangan (Yachou-fu), which districts must therefore be considered the mother colonies of its cultivation. The best tea produced in Mingshan-hsien, and indeed in Western Ssŭch'uan, grows on the Mêng-shan, a mountain 15 li (5 miles) to the West of the district city. On the summit of the mountain stands a Buddhist temple, and the priests who attend on the idol, are also the guardians of a small plantation said to contain seven shrubs

nly. Tradition has it that these shrubs were planted
uring the latter Han dynasty by a pilgrim named Wu
.ichên, who brought the seeds from India (Hsi-yü).
'he tea produced by this plantation, amounting
ɔ a few pounds only, is picked annually in the pre-
ɛnce of the territorial officials and forwarded as
:ibute to Peking. It is called *hsien-ch'a* or *kung-
h'a*. A tea, known as *Mêng-ch'a*, and reputed very
ood, is also grown elsewhere on the mountain, and is
ɔld to visitors. I have mentioned these curious facts
ecause they seem to point to an early introduction
f the tea plant from the West, and to confirm the
egative conclusion we have arrived at respecting the
resence of wild tea in Western Ssŭch'uan.

It is a popular saying that, in order to get a first
ate cup of tea, you must take "leaves from the Mêng-
ɪan, and water from the Yangtzŭ". Now, whereas
ɪe Ssŭch'uanese have no difficulty in placing the
Iêng-shan, they are all adrift about the Yangtzŭ, and,
reposterous as it may seem, I have often been asked
I had ever come across a river of that name in my
·avels. Setting aside the much debated question as
ɔ the origin of the name yangtzŭ and the range of
s applicability, it is obvious that for the purpose
lluded to the ordinary river water can not be meant.
Vhere then is the famous Yangtzŭ water to be found?
take leave to conclude this Introductory chapter
·ith a reminiscence of my own which may possibly
ɪggest an answer. Whilst residing at Shanghai I
ad occasion to pay a visit to the magistrate of that

city. I was entertained with tea which I pronounced excellent, whereupon my host dilated upon the necessity of using good water for its preparation, and added that he himself used none but Yangtzŭ water. I enquired whence he obtained it, and was told that it was brought down from Chinkiang by the daily steamer. Some time afterwards,— I had almost forgotten the incident, — I visited Chinkiang, and happened to cross over the bay which divides the foreign settlement from Golden Island, when I saw a number of small boats pull out into deep water, the crews fill their buckets, and return to the shore. I made enquiry and was informed that there was a famous spring at the bottom of the stream, which had been known ever since a time when the bed of the river was dry land. I forget the name of the spring, but it was said that a stone tablet with an ancient inscription had been standing by its side, and had been removed to an other spring farther inland, when the Yangtzŭ began to wash over the old site. The new spring has since inherited some of the celebrity of the old; but those conversant with its history are not thereby deceived, and continue to draw their water for tea drinking purposes from "the bed of the Yangtzŭ."

GENERAL AND HISTORICAL.

Tea is grown very extensively in Ssŭch'uan, and it appears that, with the exception of the mountainous regions bordering on Tibet, it is cultivated with equal success in the North, South, East, and West. No doubt the hilly configuration, good soil, and mild climate to which Ssŭch'uan owes its general prosperity, are also the conditions most favourable to the plantation of the tea shrub, the successful cultivation of which is one of the many resources which make the vaunted independence and self-sufficiency of the province in point of supplies more than an idle boast.

In point of quality, Ssŭch'uan tea does not seem to take a high rank, for none is exported abroad, except to Tibet, and even in the home market Yünnan *(P'uêrh)* tea obtains a large sale, being considered superior to the native produce, and patronised by all the better classes. After paying an Import duty of Taels 0.40 (1s. 2d.) * per pecul (133⅓ ℔s.) at Hsüchoufu, and the same at Chungking, [the Yünnan article sells at the latter place for about Taels 27 (94s. 6d.)

---

* The Tael is calculated as equivalent to 1500 cash, and to 3s. 6d. The pecul = 100 catties = 133⅓ English ℔s. The duty according to tariff is Taels 0.70 per load (140 catties), but a discount of 20 per cent being made, it is actually only Taels 0.56 per load or 0.40 per pecul. The wholesale price is Taels 38 per load or about Taels 27 per pecul.

per pecul (say 8½d. per ℔.), while the best native leaf, produced in Nanch'uan,† costs only 320 cash a catty (say 6¾d. per ℔.).   These figures are instructive when compared with the price of the "brick tea" prepared for the Tibetan market.   It is estimated that Yünnan tea is imported to the extent of about 1400 peculs (186,666 ℔s.), ‡ but a certain quantity also finds its way into Western Ssŭch'uan by the Chiench'ang route which comes out at Yachou-fu.

The quantity of tea produced annually in Ssŭch'uan is a question more of theoretical interest perhaps than of practical value.   Accurate statistics are furnished by the provincial topography, but that useful and voluminous compendium has unfortunately not been revised since the year 1815, and its figures are therefore no longer true.   A few notices respecting the earlier history of the tea trade and administration may be, however, not without interest and are extracted hereunder.

· Tea began to be taxed during the T'ang dynasty, a

---

† The best Nanch'uan tea, called *pe-hao*, costs 320 cash a catty (wholesale); the second best, called *mao-chien*, costs 200 cash a catty.   There are cheaper kinds ranging down to as low as 40 cash a catty, which is the price paid for the so called *lao-kên*, made up of twigs and refuse.   We shall come across that term again later on.

‡ 1000 loads *(tan)* of 32 barrels *(t'ung)* each.   A barrel contains 7 cakes *(yuan)*, weighing 10 ounces.   A load is therefore equivalent to 140 catties.

tithe of 10 per cent on the production, payable in kind, being levied from the year 780. During the Sung the trade was made illegal, and in three provinces only (among them Ssŭch'uan) it continued lawful within the limits of the province. In 1074 the system of bartering tea for Tibetan horses on government account was begun in Shàn-hsi, and this is the *earliest mention of the tea trade with Tibet*. This trade, however, remained a government monopoly, and public bazaars were now established in all the more important tea districts for the better control of sales and the collection of the tithe. In order to obviate the necessary but inconvenient fluctuations of the collection, a new system was subsequently devised, the yield estimated, the plantations rated, and the tithe fixed accordingly. But this manner of assessment was so arbitrary, so open to abuse, and the tax became so burdensome that a reform became necessary before long. It was undertaken in 1127, when a system of permits, to accompany and protect the goods en route, was introduced, and clandestine conveyance more efficiently checked. This was the *beginning of the permit system*, which has remained in force ever since. As early as the Ming dynasty we read about a coarse kind of tea, known as *chien-tao ts'u-ch'a*, produced in Tiao-mên (now T'iench'uan-chou) and other places, and which none but the Hsi-fan used. The Hsi-fan are the Tibetans of to-day. They used to bring their horses from Ch'angho-hsi (now Tachienlu) to Aichou-wei (now Yachou-fu), where they exchanged them for tea, a colt fetching 70 catties, the best horse 120 catties. During Yunglo (1403 to 1425) the purchase of horses was discontinued in Ssŭch'uan, but was still carried on in Shànhsi whither the tea surrendered to the government was transported. The long transport, however, caused much of the tea to arrive in bad condition, and an order was therefore issued to levy only one third of the quantity due in kind, and to accept payment in money for the other two thirds. This is the *first instance of cash payments of tea duties.* In 1569, finally, all tea duties of the province were made payable in silver. So far, when we have spoken of tea duties, the original tax or tithe on the production was always understood. When the government monopoly was abolished, and the tea trade thrown open to merchants, a tea duty *(shui)* was levied in addition to the original tithe *(k'o)*, and at the beginning of the present dynasty Taels 45,942 were collected annually on account of the former, and Taels 13,128 on account of the latter. In 1696 sanction was obtained for making *Tachienlu* the market where Tibetans accredited by the Talai-lama were allowed to carry on trade, and to make their purchases of tea. In 1719 *Lit'ang* and *Pat'ang* were admitted to the same privilege. In 1743 the system of taxation was again revised, the *permit (yin) fixed at 100 catties* (plus an allowance for waste of 14 per cent) and the tea tax *(k'o)* raised to Taels 0.125 for every permit. The number of permits was successively increased, a reserve of 5000 blank permits deposited with the Governor General, and in 1815, when the Topography breaks off, the production and distribution stood as follows :

The annual issue of permits was fixed at 139,354, of which 92,327 were export permits *(pien yin)*, 31,120 border permits *(t'u yin)*, and 15,907 inland permits *(fu yin)*. The export permits were again distributed as follows, viz., 53,004 permits filled up by the Yangan, Jung-ching and Mingshan districts, and 20,300 permits filled up in Ch'iung-chou : in all 73,304 permits were for export viâ Tachienlu; and 16,346 permits, filled up by various districts, were for export viâ Sungp'an, while 2,677 more were nominally issued for Sungp'an, but were withheld and disposed of inland. The border permits were for the supply of the more proximate native principalities *(t'u ssŭ)* on this side of the two frontier towns named, and the inland permits were, as their name indicates, for the internal trade.

Each permit was subject to four kinds of charges, viz., (a) the original tithe *(k'o)* Taels 0.125 per permit of every description ; (b) the tea duty *(shui)* Taels 0.472 for export permits, Taels 0.361 for border permits, and Taels 0.250 for inland permits ; (c) a surplus charge *(hsien-yü)* for administration expenses, Taels 0.124 for export permits, Taels 0.111 for border permits, and Taels 0.098 for inland permits ; and (d) a fee *(ch'ie-kuo)* for barrier expenses, Taels 0.142 for export permits, if filled up by the Yangan, Jungching or Mingshan districts, and Taels 0.186, if filled up by · Ch'iung-chou, for Tachienlu ; Taels 0.100, if for Sungp'an, and Taels 0.142, if Sungp'an permits disposed of internally; Taels 0.122 for border permits, and Taels 0.120 for inland permits.

The Revenue in 1815 was therefore as under:

Export permits.

T	92,327 @ 0.125		Taels	11,540.875
D	@ 0.472		,,	43,578.344
S C	@ 0.124		,,	11,448.548
F	53,004 @ 0.142 } Tachienlu		,,	7,526,568
	20,300 @ 0.186		,,	3,775.800
	16,346 @ 0.100 } Sungp'an		,,	1,634.600
	2,677 @ 0.142		,,	380.134
			Taels	79,884.869

Border permits.

T	31,120 @ 0.125		Taels	3,890.000
D	@ 0.361		,,	11,234.320
S C	@ 0.111		,,	3,454.320
F	@ 0.122		,,	3,796.640
			Taels	22,375.280

Inland permits.

T	15,907 @ 0.125		Taels	1,988.375
D	@ 0.250		,,	3,976.750
S C	@ 0.098		,,	1,558.886
F	@ 0.120		,,	1,908.840
			Taels	9,432.851

Total Tea Revenue (1815)	Taels 111,693.000

The distribution of tea showed the following percentages: Export 66, Border 22, Inland 12, while from a revenue point of view the export trade contributed 72 per cent, the supply of native principalities 20 per cent., and the home trade only 8 per cent. of the total collection. Quantitatively, *Tachienlu participated with 79 per cent*, Sungp'an with 21 per cent, *in the export trade;* the former *with 53 per cent*, the latter with 14 per cent, *in the whole tea trade of the province*. Tachienlu contributed *Taels 64,154.552*, Sungp'an Taels 15,730.317, to the above revenue. In the following the export trade viâ Tachienlu will occupy us alone.

ADMINISTRATION AND REVENUE.

When compared with the foregoing statistics,—and considering that three quarters of a century have elapsed since they were made,—the figures for the present tea trade at Tachienlu, and for the revenue now collected, show a great, but not an abnormal development.

The Tea and Salt Commissioner *(yen-ch'a tao)* resident at Ch'êngtu is the head of the administration under the Governor General. The permits, under which the trade is carried on, are issued annually by the Board of Revenue in Peking, and are returned to it at the end of the year. The number of permits allotted to Tachienlu for export North and West is

108,000.   After receiving the impression of the Governor General's seal, they are transmitted by the Tea Commissioner to the Sub-prefect *(t'ing,* also styled *chünliang fu,* because in charge of the Commissariat), who is the highest civil officer at Tachienlu. The latter is assisted by two special Deputies *(wei-yuan),* and the three officers are jointly responsible for the collection of the revenue.   The permits are given out in the second Chinese moon, and called in in the tenth moon, and any deficiency then existing must be made good, the blank permits being surrendered and cancelled like those filled up.   The dues and duties payable on each permit aggregate Taels 1.10, and the revenue accruing to the central government from the tea trade at Tachienlu is therefore *Taels 118,800* per annum.   For this sum the Tea Commissioner is supposed to be accountable to the Board of Revenue.

Beside the above regular or ordinary permits *(yin* or *chêng-yin),* special permits *(p'iao)* are issued by the Tea Commissioner.   They are intended to provide against the contingency of a deficit; but, since the regular permits are always entirely taken up, the dues collected on these special permits have really become a perquisite of the Tea Commissioner.   One special permit is issued for every ten regular ones, that is, 10,800 per annum.   They cover the same quantity of tea, but the dues and duties amount to only Taels 0.80 a piece, and they realise therefore Taels 8.640 per annum.

Similarly 5,000 more permits *(ên-p'iao)* are issued annually by the Sub-prefect, to ensure himself against loss, and 3,000 for the benefit of the two Deputies. These permits pay at the same rate as the last, and realise Taels 6,400 per annum.

The total number of permits issued every year, and the actual collection of dues and duties on tea at Tachienlu is as under :

O P	108,000	@ 1.10	Taels	118,800
S P	10,800	@ 0.80	,,	8,640
	5,000	@ 0.80	,,	4,000
	3,000	@ 0.80	,,	2,400
	126,800		Taels	133,840

As a set off against the above facts it should be mentioned that the central government allows only the modest sum of Taels 840 per annum for cost of the tea administration at Tachienlu. This sum provides for salaries of Taels 300 a year to each of the two deputies, and of Taels 60 a year each to four clerks, while the maintenance of a dozen or so of servants and runners found by the Sub-prefect, and other incidental expenses in connection with the tea office are not provided for.

DISTRIBUTION OF PERMITS.

The Sub-prefect of Tachienlu receives applications for permits from the Magistrates of the five districts which enjoy the privilege of supplying the tea for the Tibetan market.   In his turn the Magistrate of each district opens a list of applicants for tea permits in the second moon every year.   In order to obtain these, merchants must find sureties amongst the respectable and substantial residents of the district; and, as the trade is a highly profitable one, and competition therefore keen, a considerable outlay is usually connected, in the first place, with the finding of the sureties, and, in the next, with getting them accepted. When the matter has been satisfactorily arranged, the successful applicants are furnished by the Magistrate with documents on presentation of which the permits are issued by the Sub-prefect of Tachienlu. The permits are transferable, and do sometimes become an article of trade in themselves; but the original owner remains responsible for the dues payable on them.   All tea transported to Tachienlu must be accompanied by permits, and the latter are inspected both at Luting-ch'iao and at the city gates of Tachienlu.   But the duties are paid only after sale, when the permits also are surrendered.

The distribution of the permits amongst the five privileged districts is according to the following fixed ratio :

Ch'iung-chou	27,000
Mingshan-hsien	8,000
T'iench'uan-chou	23,000
Yangan-hsien	27,000
Jungching-hsien	23,000
Total, regular permits	108,000

The distribution of the special permits is not bound by any rule.

PRODUCTION.

Each permit covers five packages *(pao)*. The packages being not exactly uniform, the quantity of tea annually exported viâ Tachienlu is a matter for nice calculation. We will here anticipate, what will be made apparent hereafter, that the 126,800 permits annually issued represent *peculs 108,780*.

The five districts enumerated are not capable of producing the entire quantity locally, and three more districts are therefore allowed to participate in the supply of the raw material, viz. Ch'ingch'i-hsien, Omei-hsien, and Hungya-hsien. The share taken by each district in the production of tea for the Tachienlu market is in round figures as follows:

Ch'iung-chou	peculs	19,000
Mingshan	,,	22,000
T'iench'uan	,,	20,000
Yangan	,,	12,000
Jungching	,,	9,000
Ch'ingch'i	,,	7,000
Omei	,,	8,000
Hungya	,,	13,000
Total	peculs	110,000

Ch'iung-chou is an independent sub-prefecture; Hungya and Omei belong to the prefecture of Chiating, all the other districts to that of Yachou. Ch'ingch'i and Omei convey their produce to Jungching; Hungya to Yangan.

The manufacture of the tea for the Tibetan market, and the trade, however, are confined to the five districts first enumerated, and the quantity of raw material available to each of these is as under:

	Local.	Imported.	Total.
Ch'iung-chou	19,000		19,000
Mingshan	22,000		22,000
T'iench'uan	20,000		20,000
Yangan	12,000	13,000	25,000
Jungching	9,000	15,000	24,000
Total		peculs	110,000

It must not be supposed that this is all genuine tea; it will be seen, on the contrary, that real tea constitutes but the smallest part of the material employed in the manufacture of tea bricks.

CULTIVATION.

The growing of tea plants for seed is confined to the districts of Mingshan and Yangan. The seed is sold by the measure, not by weight, the *tou* selling for 400 cash. The art of planting the shrub, and of laying out tea gardens is likewise a monopoly of the tea planters of the two districts named, and these men are hired for that purpose by all the tea growers of the neighbouring districts. The seed is put into the ground within ten days of the *yüshui* period (about 19th February). A hill slope, not too elevated neither too low, is usually selected, and small handfuls of the seed are buried in rows, some two feet apart. But I have also seen plants growing as borders to fields, or dotted in irregular clusters about the farm houses. The labour is not paid for at once, but only after the lapse of three years, and it is then paid for according to results, that is to say, if one, two, three, or four plants only are found alive in one cluster after that period, no remuneration is due; but if five or more plants are found alive, then one cash is paid for each plant. Nine or ten is the greatest number of plants ever found in one cluster.

The tea shrubs which, during the earlier stages of

growth, generally share the soil with some other produce, mostly maize, ordinarily attain to a height of 2
or 3 feet, and seldom reach to a man's shoulder.
They are left much to themselves until they are four
years old when the first crop is taken.   The picking
commences in February and ceases in June.   It proceeds progressively downwards from the top.   The
young buds and tips *(chien)* form the first and finest
crop; the young but fullgrown leaves the second *(hsi-
ch'a)*, and the coarser foliage the third crop *(ts'u-ch'a)*.
The picking is continued for three years, after which
the plants cease to sprout, and when therefore they
are cut down, stem, branches and all, to make room
for a new plantation.   This last crop is known as
lao-kên.   On larger plantations, where home labour
is insufficient, extra pickers are hired who earn, beside
food and lodging, one cash per catty of 18 ounces.
There is no restriction to the planting or growing of
tea, nor is the preparation of the leaf for home use
or market, or the sale thereof within the district at
all interfered with.   The better qualities are very
carefully prepared, but find no sale in non-Chinese
territories, and are either consumed locally, or traded
in under inland permits.   The local market quotations
are as under:

	Wholesale.	Retail.
1st Quality	Cash 320 per catty	Cash 420 per catty
2nd ,,	,, 240 ,,	,, 320 ,,
3rd ,,	,, 180 ,,	,, 220 ,,

a catty being always equivalent to 18 ounces in the tea trade.   I quote these prices in order to show that the very lowest of them is more than five times the value of the tea made into "bricks" for consumption in Tibet and elsewhere. *

For the manufacture of the so called "brick tea" for Tibet, the first and second qualities are not employed at all, and the third quality enters into it to a very limited extent.   The bulk of the material is made up of the *lao-kên*, consisting of stems, branches, and the coarsest of leaves only, admixed with a great quantity of twigs and branches of certain other trees and shrubs, such as the scrub oak *(ch'ing-kang)*, a vitex *(huang-ching)*, a tree called *chüan-tzŭ*, and others, which are not planted at all, but the branches of which are simply cut off and collected like brushwood in the forests.   This brushwood is known as *ye-kên*, and is collected all the year round.   Generally the tea planters who sell the lao-kên, supply the

---

* To declare, as some have done, that the Chinese keep all the better teas for themselves, and supply the merest refuse to the Tibetans whom they regard as savages who know no better, is, I need hardly point out, a shortsighted view to take.   The Chinese, so far as I know them, would be only too glad to sell to the Tibetans, or to any other savages, whatever these will pay for.   It has never before been clearly shown how dirt cheap the stuff is, which the Tibetans drink, compared even with very common Chinese tea.   Moreover, it seems really as if the Tibetans did not care for better teas, even if they could pay for them.

ye-kên also. Both are stacked in the open air, like firewood, until dried by the sun. They are sold by the bundle *(k'un)*, the lao-kên weighing 160 catties of 32 or 33 ounces each per bundle, the ye-kên 178 catties of 33 or 34 ounces each per bundle. The former sells for 32 cash a catty, the latter for 12 or 13 cash a catty. As the farmers have neither the knowledge of, nor the appliances for, preparing the tea for export, the material is sold to the factories. The transport to the latter, calculated at the rate of 3 cash a bundle for every li, is defrayed by the buyers.

MANUFACTURE.

The country produce having been bought up and conveyed to town, is prepared in the factories for the Tibetan market. The process of preparation as I saw it in Yachou-fu is exceedingly simple. The lao-kên and the ye-kên are both chopped fine, and dried once more in that state. They are then mixed in a certain proportion and steamed in large wooden tubs. The mass is spread out on clean mats, and, when superficially dry, rice water *(chiang)* is added to it in sufficient quantity to make it adhesive. When thoroughly stirred the "tea" is now ready for packing. The packing is done in this manner. First a number of small parcels are made, containing 4 ounces of tea of a better quality, and done up in red paper. Sheets of bamboo matting of the proper length and breadth have been got ready in the meantime, and pasted over on the inside with ordinary white paper. They are rolled into the shape of a cylinder, and one end being closed up with one of the red parcels described, the tea mixture is packed in tightly from the other. The package is finally closed up with a second parcel in red paper, and the mat covering sewn up. *

There are two kinds of packages *(pao)* turned out, one of a trifling better quality, i.e., with a somewhat larger proportion of tea in it, weighing about 16 catties; and the other of inferior quality weighing about 18 catties. The former kind is destined for exportation to the native principalities Northwest of Tachienlu; the latter for exportation to Lit'ang, Pa-t'ang, and Tibet proper. The cost per package of the two qualities is exactly the same, the superiority in quality of the one being compensated for by the larger weight of the other.

It is calculated that about 35 per cent of cultivated tea, and 65 per cent of brushwood enter into the composition of the tea exported viâ Tachienlu, and that the mixture costs the manufacturer, inclusive of prime cost, transport to factory, labour of chopping, steaming, &c., but exclusive of packing, 32 cash a catty (about two thirds of a penny a ℔.)

---

* In Jungching, apparently, according to Mr. Baber, the tea is not hand packed, but pressed in wooden moulds. I have not seen that process myself, nor any of the "bricks" turned out by it.

An expert packer requires no scales, but will pack exactly 16, resp. 18, catties into one package. The remuneration of the men employed in steaming and packing, which is considered skilled labour, is 100 cash, that of the men employed in stoking, chopping, preparing the starch, and sewing the packages, is 60 cash per diem. The workmen are divided in six classes, and there is strict division of labour. The mat covering for each package costs 40 cash, and the paper lining 12 cash.

All the tea prepared in the manner detailed is taken to Tachienlu for sale. The term "brick" so frequently applied to it, is, as has been pointed out, quite inappropriate. The package resembles a brick neither in shape nor in consistency. It has been said that it should be called brick *(chuan)* only after it has been cut in two, as is sometimes done at Tachienlu for convenience of transport. But I have just as often seen the original packages leave Tachienlu, especially by the Northern route.

TRANSPORT.

There are two roads from Yachou-fu to Tachienlu. The main road runs Southwest to Jungching, thence across the Tahsiang-ling to Ch'ingch'i and again across the Feiyüe-ling to Hualin-p'ing, where it strikes the valley of the Taitu-ho. It follows the left bank of that river Northwards to Luting-ch'iao, a small but busy settlement, where all the traffic from and to Tachienlu makes halt. The iron suspension bridge which spans the river at this place, is the only connection between the right and the left bank of the Taitu-ho above its Eastward bend, and navigation is impossible for all ordinary craft, owing to the strong current of the river.* Luting ch'iao is therefore an important barrier. After crossing the bridge, the right bank is followed North to the entrance of the Lu-ho, where the road turns West and follows that stream to Tachienlu.

The smaller and shorter road goes from Yachou Westnorthwest to T'iench'uan, and thence almost due West across two not very high, but exceedingly steep mountain ranges which probably connect with those met with on the Southern route, until finally it comes out on the left bank of the Taitu-ho, some 10 li above Luting-ch'iao. Although shorter than the

---

* The natives (Tibetans) use coracles. With the aid of this light and primitive craft they cross the swiftest current easily and safely. Shaped like a nutshell, but rather wider at the bottom than round the edge, the coracle *(p'i-ch'uan)* consists of a stout wooden frame over which the raw hide of a buffalo or yak is tightly drawn. The inconsiderable weight is essential, but the real secret of the construction lies in the distribution of the weight, which is all at the bottom of the boat, where the people taking passage crouch, or which may be ballasted with stones. At the end of the journey the coracle is easily lifted unto a man's shoulder and carried along until again required.

main road, this route is much more toilsome, and for
heavily laden porters the time occupied in the journey
is very nearly the same, though, if travelling without
baggage, two days can be gained between Tachienlu
and Yachou.

The distances to Tachienlu from each of the manu-
facturing towns are as follows :

Ch'iung-chou	Short route	510 li.
Mingshan	Long ,,	570 ,,.
Yangan	,, ,,	540 ,,
T'iench'uan	,, ,.	480 ,,
Jungching	,, ,,	450 ,,

It is optional for porters to take whichever route
they prefer.   The portage is reckoned per permit (of
5 packages), and is noted hereunder.   But it must be
explained that these fees are nominal only and are
subject in each case to a deduction of 20 per cent.
This is expressed by the term *pa ts'e suan*.   One half
of the portage is paid in advance, the other half on
delivery.

	Nominal.	Actual.
Ch'iung-chou	Taels 1.30	Taels 1.04
Mingshan	,, 1.70	,, 1.36
Yangan	,, 1.30	,. 1.04
T'iench'uan	,, 1.10	,, 0.88
Jungching	,, 0.90	,, 0.72

An able bodied man is said to be capable of carrying
the equivalent of three permits (15 packages = 240
to 270 catties, or 320 to 360 ℔s.), but from my own

experience I should have judged 11 or 12 packages (250 to 280 ℔s.) to be the usual quantity carried by a grown up person.   The manner in which these porters proceed en route has been frequently described and depicted.

On arrival at Luting-ch'iao the goods are examined, and the permits inspected and stamped by the Assistant Magistrate *(hsün-chien-ssŭ* or *you-t'ang)* of that place. A fee of 18 cash per permit is collected for this office. The porters do not carry their heavy loads across the bridge themselves, but these are unstrung, and the packages carried across one by one, by a special class of men who are always in attendance.   One cash per package is paid for this service.   After crossing the bridge the porters readjust their burdens and continue their journey to Tachienlu.   The incidental expenses enumerated are borne by the owners, and are not included in the portage.

SALE.

On entering Tachienlu the tea is tallied and registered by one of the Deputies at the city gate.   It is then taken to one of the warehouses *(c'ha-tien)* where it awaits sale.   There are 36 Chinese warehouses in the city, and 48 packing establishments *(kuo-chuang)* which are Tibetan.   The merchants who do a large amount of business usually have their own warehouses, while others are obliged to make temporary use of those existing, and in that case one cash is paid for storage *(fang-huo-ch'ien)*.   There are yet other merchants who, having secured permits, do not possess the capital for doing business themselves, and who loan their permits to second parties.   Taels 200 are usually paid for this friendly act for every 1000 permits, besides all charges payable thereon to the government.

The Tibetans who live in the kuo-chuang pay neither rent nor storage, board or lodging, but it is understood that the proprietors of these establishments receive a commission of 8 per cent on every business transaction which takes place on their premises.   The buying is done almost entirely by women, the men being the while pressed into service by the native chief of the principality in which Tachienlu is situated, who is styled Mingchêng t'u-ssû, and is sometimes erroneously called "the king of Tachienlu" by foreign writers.

When a purchase has been made, the tea is sometimes repacked.   The mat covering is in that case removed, and the solid contents cut into two " bricks " which are encased in hide casings.   This work is performed by a special class of men, who receive no remuneration beyond the cast off matting and the two small parcels in red, containing 8 ounces of tea.

The seller proceeds to the Deputy's office, and surrenders the permits for the quantity of tea sold, paying at the same time the amount due thereon.

The price paid at Tachienlu for each package, large

or small, is Rupees 5, and this value is subject to hardly any fluctuation. As stated before, the smaller and somewhat superior packages are exported to the native principalities Northwest of Tachienlu (Gata, Tawu, Horchangku, Derge, &c.). They leave Tachienlu by the North gate, and amount to *53,400 permits* annually. The larger packages of inferior quality are for export to Lit'ang, Pat'ang, and Tibet proper. They leave Tachienlu by the West gate, and represent *73,400 permits* per annum.

Tachienlu is situated at the confluence of the two head waters of the Lu-ho, the Dar and the Ché, whence the name Darchédo, of which Tachienlu is obviously a corruption. The Dar springs from the Cheto (Jeddo) pass, Southwest of Tachienlu, and on the main road to Tibet, whilst the Ché-ch'u (ch'u is a stream) descends from the Haitzŭ-shan, Northwest of Tachienlu, on the route to Ch'inghai (Kokonoor). Little was known about this route until in 1889 Mr. Rockhill accomplished the journey, although he was not the first foreigner to have performed it, having been preceded by the Pundit A————k, an intrepid Hindu in the employ of the Trigonometral Survey department of India.

Chinese tea merchants do not venture beyond Tachienlu. In the Northwestern principalities tea seems to be largely bought on behalf of the native chieftains tributary to China; whilst in Tibet proper the priesthood appear to monopolise the trade entirely. In this connection I was informed that a custom which contributes largely to the consumption of tea in Tibetan countries is the free distribution of the *"su-ch'a"* ("buttered tea") on certain festival days, notably on the 20th of the 10th Chinese moon.   I have no doubt the "general teas" or "mang ja", mentioned by Rockhill (Op. cit. p. 104) must be meant.

S U M M A R Y.

We are only now in possession of all the facts necessary for calculating with any degree of precision the quantity of tea annually exported viâ Tachienlu, and the value of that trade.

We have seen (p. 18 f.) that the whole trade is represented by 108,000 *regular permits*, and 18,800 *special permits*, in all by 126,800 parmits; that the duty paid on each regular permit is Taels 1.10, and on each special permit Taels 0.80; that the collection of duties on the former is therefore Taels 118,800, on the latter Taels 15,040, and the *total collection* Taels 133,840 per annum.

We have seen (p. 33) that the equivalent of 73,400 permits is reexported from Tachienlu to the *West*, and the equivalent of 53,400 permits to the *North;* that, while each permit covers 5 packages, the packages are not uniform in weight, those going West weighing 18 catties, those going North 16 catties each.   The permits for the Western trade therefore represents 90 catties, that for the Northern trade 80 catties ; and we have as the

Total quantity of tea exported viâ Tachienlu

73,400 permits	@ 0,90 =	peculs	66,060	West
53,400 ,,	@ 0.80 =	,,	42,720	North
Total		peculs	108,780	

The first of these figures, peculs 66,060, or ℔s. 8,808,000, covers not only the whole supply of Tibet proper, but that also of the principalities of Lit'ang and Pat'ang.

We have seen (p. 27) that the above quantity is made up of 35 per cent of *cultivated tea* of the lowest class, and of 65 per cent of *wild shrubs*. The proportion of these two constituents is therefore as under

Cultivated tea	35%	peculs	38,073
Wild shrubs	65%	,,	70,707
Total		peculs	108,780

For the places of production and the distribution of permits I refer to p. 22 and 21 respectively

We have seen (p. 27) that the cost price of the manufactured article, exclusive of packing is Cash 32 per catty, and we have therefore to set down for

Prime Cost.

Peculs 108,780 @ 32 cash a catty = (1,000) 348,096 @ 0.80 = Taels 278,476.80.

For packing, toll at Luting-ch'iao, and other incidental expenses it is calculated that cash 66 per package, or cash 330 per permit are paid.   We have thus for

Packing, &c.,

126,800 permits @ 330 cash = (1000) 41,844 @ 0.80 = Taels 33,475.20

Taking as our basis Yachou-fu, whence the portage to Tachienlu is nominally Taels 1.30, actually only Taels 1.04, per permit, we get for

Transport,

126,800 permits @ 1.04 =   Taels 131,872.

Adding to this the amount payable for

Dues and Duties,

Taels 133,840,

we obtain as the

Net value of the trade,

that is, of the tea, laid down at Tachienlu, duty paid, but *exclusive of profits,*

Taels 576,864,

In order to obtain the

Gross Value (incl. of profits),

we have only to multiply the number of packages by five, to get the value in Rupees which exchange for Taels 0.32 of silver, thus

126,800 permits @ 5 = packages 634,000 @ 5 = Rupees 3,170,000, @ 0.32 =

Taels 1,014,400.

The *profit* annually made in the trade is therefore

Taels 437,536, a result which is in perfect accord with the statement I have heard made that an investment ¯of Taels 20,000 will return from Taels 35,000 to 36,000. It is evident from this that the privilege to participate in the trade is a valuable one, and one not easily obtained; and it is apparent also why the permits are always taken up so eagerly and to their full margin.

CONCLUSION.

I was told by an official well acquainted with Tibetan affairs that the principal objection to the opening up of Tibet on the Indian side is the loss to China of the tea trade, which would inevitably follow. With less information at my command, I am yet inclined to challenge that oft repeated apprehension.

In the first place it is questionable whether the aversion which is said to be now professed by Tibetans to the stronger Indian beverage can be overcome, whether it is not more than mere habit, and whether the Indian tea would "take" in that country.

We must give our consideration, in the next place, to the *point of cost*. We have seen that the package weighing 18 catties is sold at Tachienlu for Rupees 5, or (@ 0.32) Taels 1.60, that is, at the rate of Taels 8.88 a pecul. The last value is equivalent to about, $2\frac{3}{4}$d. a ℔. This, it will be remembered, includes about 75 per cent profit, a rate of interest capable, it will be

admitted, of some reduction.   In any case, for purposes of comparison, we must take not this, but the
net value, which we have seen to be, for duty paid tea
laid down at Tachienlu, $\frac{576,864}{108,780}$ or Taels 5.30 a pecul.
This value is equivalent to about 1½d. a ℔.   The same
tea we have seen to be worth, at place of production,
32 cash a catty, or less than 3 farthings a ℔.   Is it
possible to produce anywhere in India tea that will
compete for cheapness with the stuff, now sold as tea
to, and so highly prized by, the Tibetans?   Moreover,
if Indian tea is even admitted into Tibet, it will probably be subject to some sort of duty, and, no matter
whether the Tachienlu rate be adopted, which is about
52d. a pecul, or the maritime tariff, which is about as
much again (105d.), the tea would have to cost little
more than a penny a ℔. to compete with the present
article in point of cost.

Our next consideration will be the *cost of transport*.
It may be thought that, where distances are shorter, a
saving in carriage will enable Indian teas to compete
with the " brick tea " of China, and, with certain limit-
ations, this may be true.   According to M. Desgodins
(La Mission du Thibet p. 300), it would appear that
the transport from Tachienlu to Pat'ang about doubles
the price, trebles it at Ch'amuto, and quadruples it at
Lasa.   If this is so, the package of 18 catties would
be worth Rup. 20 at Lasa, that is 11d. a ℔.   It is for
the commercial world of India to ascertain whether
their teas could be laid down in Lasa at that figure;
but I think that, beyond that city, that is on the Chi-

nese side of it, there is hardly any danger of their competition, for, in proportion as their prices would advance, the Chinese prices would fall. What is here contended for, is not, that Indian tea may not be introduced with advantage into the ulterior parts of Tibet, but that Chinese tea will maintain itself in the proximate. In this opinion I am glad to find more that I am supported by Mr. Baber, whose remarks at the end of his valuable paper (R. G. S. Supplementary Papers Vol. I. Part I. p. 199) are highly instructive. It is also pointed out by that author that the supply of tea in Tibet falls much short of the demand, and that the trade is therefore capable of great development. His remarks become even more forcible when it is observed that his estimate of the tea supply going to Tibet proper is rather too high although considerably below the total for the trade at Tachienlu, because the quantity going to the Northern principalities seems to have escaped his notice. The Tibetan trade, including that of Lit'ang and Pat'ang, we have seen to be under 9 million ℔s., and it represents at Tachienlu a value of Rupees 1,835,000, or £ 102,760. That figure, I should think, would hardly be affected by Indian competition, and the " tea question " as put in the opening of this concluding chapter, is to my mind either a delusion or a blind.

There is one point, however, which does not seem to have occurred to any of the writers on the subject, and which may yet be worthy of a passing notice. Commodities so necessary to a state as tea and salt, may, if the supply thereof be monopolised by any one country, become a powerful lever for maintaining the political influence in that country. Without distinctly formulating that principle, the Chinese seem to have acted upon it. They have not forced their produce upon the Tibetans, but have conceded to them as a privilege that they might come and purchase it at their frontier towns ; and this privilege has even been withdrawn once or twice, temporarily, in the case of principalities which had proved refractory. Again, instead of flooding the country with tea as we should be inclined to do, the Chinese have limited the supply and kept it below demand. The exclusive dependence on China for this important commodity seems to me a political factor not to be underrated, and I believe that, if the monopoly of the tea trade were to be done away with, much of the Chinese influence in Tibet would be gone also.

Printed in Holland.